Lorraine Bernier was born and raised in London, UK, before spending the majority of her adult life in France. Alongside writing, she enjoys nature and painting in the Garden of England, Kent.

Her first book, *The Fairy Dales of Alberton Forest*, is a combination of fairy magic and the traditional challenges that most children encounter as part of growing up.

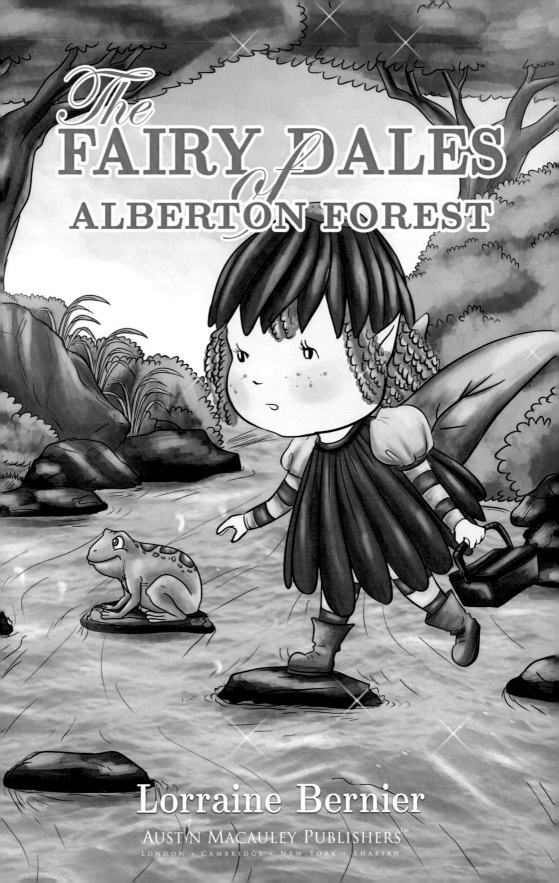

The FAIRY DALES of ALBERTON FOREST

Lorraine Bernier

AUSTIN MACAULEY PUBLISHERS™
LONDON • CAMBRIDGE • NEW YORK • SHARJAH

A CIP catalogue record for this title is available from the British Library.

ISBN 9781528927406 (Paperback)
ISBN 9781528965057 (ePub e-book)

www.austinmacauley.com

First Published (2021)
Austin Macauley Publishers Ltd
25 Canada Square
Canary Wharf
London
E14 5LQ

To my three wonderful children and my brother, Tony.

Introduction

In the centre of the mysterious and beautiful Alberton Forest, stood a very old oak tree. This tree was enchanted. Every morning, as dawn broke on the horizon and the beaming golden rays of sun fought their way through the branches, there seemed to be a ruffling, scuffling sound, all the way down to the roots at the very bottom of the tree.

At exactly six o'clock, every morning in the Forest, the air filled with the sweet aroma of rose petals. Deep down under the roots of the old enchanted oak tree was a whole new world, The Fairy Dales of Alberton Forest. This is the home of the flower, tree and fruit fairies.

On the top of the hillside in Fairy Dales, lived a very wise elderly fairy called Grandma Roseraine. She was extremely respected by all the other fairies. Her cotton-wool white, silky soft hair sat on top of her head just like a rose. Her cheeks were the rosiest, plumpest and roundest smiley cheeks ever to be seen. She wore the tiniest pair of half-moon glasses that sat perfectly on her little button nose and she wore petticoats made from layers and layers of delicate rose petals. She was normally seen at the very top of the hills, amongst the rose bushes that surrounded the old oak tree. Grandma Roseraine was a very important fairy, for when the sun awoke, she was the first fairy to rise.

Carrying her mysterious fairy dust, she, like clockwork, whizzed above all the little fairy homes, scattering behind her a glistening trail of the most delicious, distinctive scent of rose petals. Within seconds, the fairy noses were twitching, the birds were singing and the bees were buzzing. The Dales was now awake and a new day began...

Chapter 1
Grandma Roseraine and
the Comfort Tree

The morning was bright, and the sky above was as blue as the sea. The fairies bustled about excitedly in their homes selecting their finest outfits, making sure they were presentable for a special afternoon tea with Grandma Roseraine.

You see, today was Dummy Day. This meant that the time had come for the little fairies to fill their bags and give all of their old dummies to the gracious Grandma to look after. However, not all of the fairies were happy about this...

On this day, Fairy Dales had some very excited fairies, but it also had some very sad and nervous ones too. There were fairies that didn't even use their dummies anymore, so they were fine, whilst there were others that did. Grandma Roseraine was a very caring and wise fairy and she only took the old tired dummies that weren't of use anymore.

Over at Thistle Tower, Fairy Timmy Thistle was busy rinsing his dummy under warm soapy water in preparation, making sure that it sparkled clean. His dummy had gathered dust from being kept inside his sock drawer for far too long. He didn't mind giving his dummy to Grandma Roseraine. He was more excited about having cream tea and cakes with the other fairies!

On the opposite side of the Dales at Bluebell Barn, Fairy Bluebell Braie was very sad and worried. His little dummy was so precious to him. He held on so tightly to his and found it extremely difficult to put his tired and used dummy into his little bag. He definitely didn't want to hand it over to Grandma Roseraine. He just didn't understand why he couldn't keep it.

Up on the hilltop lived Grandma Roseraine, in the trunk of the very old enchanted Oak Tree that sat proudly overlooking the Fairy Dales. Fairy Roseraine was busy making puffy petal cushions for all the fairies to sit on, spreading them around her little garden in front of the enchanted old oak tree. She had already filled tiny pots with glittery fairy dust early that morning as a gift to the fairies in return for their dummies and she was preparing plenty of berry juice, cream tea and cherry cakes for them all.

As the big, blazing sun sat high up in the clear sky, the Fairy Dales bell chimed loudly. All the fairies gathered together in the town square comparing their little dummies and chatting happily. They instantly joined hands looking like a daisy chain, their little bags with their dummies attached firmly to their waists and in one jump, they all took off into the air.

They flew high over the fairy homes, making their way up to the hilltop. As they landed one after the other, they cuddled Grandma Roseraine and then sat down on the cushions of petals. The air was filled with sweet rose and it was buzzing with bees collecting the soft pollen in the surrounding flowers. Grandma's little crooked door was open as she hobbled back and forth serving juice, tea and delicious cakes to the fairies.

Once the fairies were calm and their tummies were full, Grandma Roseraine began to talk...

"Hello my lovelies. Today is a very brave and special day for all of you. I know that all of your dummies are precious and cherished. They have been with you for many fairy years. It is always a little sad when we decide to let them go. And for this, I came up with somewhere very special for them to go. So here I present to you all, the dummy tree."

The little fairies were listening carefully, as Grandma Roseraine continued.

"We shall hang all of your precious dummies on my Old Oak Tree and call it 'The Fairy Dales Comfort Tree'. I promise to take extra special care of them all."

The fairies sat listening attentively to Grandma Roseraine. They looked up at the old oak tree and imagined their dummies high in the branches.

The little fairy faces beamed. They looked at each other with mouths opened wide. They squealed and jumped in the air and started to sing as they flew around the trunk of the old oak tree.

"Up and down, how jolly are we,
Round and round the old oak tree,
Up on the hilltop standing bright,
Our dummies are bathed in love and light,

Oh, shine our precious comfort tree,
Day and night for all to see!"

Grandma Roseraine was overjoyed to see that her suggestion had caused such excitement amongst the fairies. She couldn't help but notice that one little fairy didn't seem to agree. He looked very unhappy with his head looking downwards and a rainbow coloured dummy held tightly in his mouth. His little eyebrows frowned.
Fairy Bluebell Braie did not want to leave his dummy at all. Grandma Roseraine made her way over to him and sat gracefully down beside him. She took his little hand and placed it gently into hers. Just behind his dummy, she could see his chin wobble as if he was about to cry. They softly chatted for a little while, and Bluebell Braie's face began to smile gradually.

A little pot of multi coloured fairy dust was exchanged for his precious and colourful dummy. Grandma lifted Bluebell Braie into the air and swirled around, hugging him. He was soon singing along with the other fairies...

"Flying around, how happy are we,
Round and round the old oak tree,
Up on the hilltop, day and night,
Holding our dummies oh so tight,
Oh, shine our precious Comfort Tree,
Light up the night for all to see."

The fairies then formed a queue alongside the old oak tree. One by one, they flew up into the branches to hang their dummies amongst the leaves. When the old oak tree was completely full, the little fairies joined hands, nodded to Grandma Roseraine and flew back home, down into the Dales. As soon as they landed in the town square, the bell chimed loudly and off they all flew their separate ways.

The evening came, the sun went to sleep. High up in the branches, were little cocooned homes belonging to the family of fireflies. The fireflies were very important in Fairy Dales as the elderly fireflies lit up the old oak tree at night so that it shone brightly over the Dales. The younger ones sat on little twigs to light the pathways around the Dales enabling the fairies to see in the dark. The big, bright moon rose in the dark night sky.

The fairies filled their fires with logs of wood, making sure their little homes stayed warm throughout the night. They dressed in their pyjamas and little bobble hats, snuggling down, warm and cosy into their beds.

Lying on their pillows, they could see the top of the hill where Roseraine lives through their windows and up there, glistening with lights from the fireflies and decorated with dummies of all shapes and colours, stood proud the old oak tree, twinkling bright for all to see.

This was the Fairy Dales' very own 'Comfort Tree'. The fairies closed their eyes and Fairy Dales of Alberton Forest fell deeply to sleep.

Chapter 2
Daisydimple and the Big Round Yellow Glasses

The wind was filling his cheeks and whisking warm air across the Dales. Today was Pancake Day and a heavenly day for some sugar-coated zestful ones too. The fairies were fluttering around with excitement as their tummies rumbled, gurgled and grumbled from their dinky noses detecting the sweet aroma.

Fairies Daisydimple and Blandine Buttercup lived in Oak View Cottages at the bottom of the hill not far from the valley town square. This year, they were chosen by Grandma Roseraine to make pancakes for all the fairies and it was for Daisydimple to gather together the ingredients in preparation for cooking whilst Blandine Buttercup carefully picked fresh lemons from the valley lemon tree.

But Daisydimple wasn't preparing anything in her little house. Something was bothering her. Earlier that morning, a friendly, chirpy sparrow had delivered her a small package with her name written boldly across the front. Daisydimple sat herself down, spread her apron across her knees and proceeded to carefully open the package.

18

She was a rather cute, plump fairy with big black curls that fell around her dimply cheeks. Her curls would bounce up and down when she walked. Inside the intriguing, small package was a huge, round, yellow pair of glasses. This being exactly what was bothering Daisydimple. They were Daisydimple's new glasses. She was not happy at all. They were the biggest pair of round yellow glasses she had ever seen in the land. Daisydimple slowly picked them up and despite the dread of having to wear them, she bravely placed them on her button nose. She unwantedly took a peek at herself in the mirror. They weren't at all fairylike… They were too big for her dainty fairy face… They squished her round, rosy cheeks like two oranges. They were even larger than her dainty fairy wings!

Daisydimple sat back down and dropped her head into her hands in despair. "No other fairy in all of the Fairy Dales had a pair of glasses like these!" she mumbled with a little sadness to herself.

All of the excitement for Pancake Day had sadly disappeared and Blandine was due to return rather soon with the lemons. Daisydimple did not want Blandine Buttercup to see her glasses for she will surely laugh. *How will I fly?* she thought to herself. Surely, they were too heavy.

She sighed!
Off went the big round yellow glasses and very quickly were tucked inside a little embroidered handkerchief that Daisydimple was so talented at making. She then hid them safely away inside an old wooden blanket chest in her bedroom. Daisydimple scuffled back to the unprepared kitchen and started to gather together the ingredients for pancakes. She had soon forgotten about her glasses. She hummed a jolly tune out loud as she fluttered about bumping into the furniture.

Blandine Buttercup joined in with the humming as she flew into the house and through to the kitchen with her little basket of delicious lemons. But the humming very quickly stopped.

"What on earth is wrong Daisydimple?" Blandine asked. Fairy Daisydimple was now flustered and confused. Blandine continued.

"Oh! Look here! What are these ingredients you have out? Are we not making pancakes?" she questioned. Now Daisydimple was puzzled. Surely Blandine Buttercup could see that sugar, eggs and flour were out ready to mix up for pancakes... Hmm, maybe Blandine needs glasses too! Yes! Daisydimple jumped for joy.

"Blandine Buttercup!" she exclaimed.

"You must find yourself some new glasses like mine. It is so much easier to see. You won't bump into furniture. The sky appears bluer and the flowers are prettier, and the sun shines brighter and..." Daisydimple babbled excitedly. Fairy Blandine Buttercup squidged her little face into a ball, baffled and interrupted Daisydimple.

"Daisydimple... I can see very clearly, but I am bewildered. If you have glasses, then why aren't you wearing them? These ingredients are perfect for a warm winter broth, but certainly not to make pancakes!"

Daisydimple was silent. She lowered her dainty wings and her soft curls hid her face as she bowed her head down. She then took hold of Blandine Buttercup's hand and proceeded to wobble into the bedroom. There, she opened the wooden chest and carefully took out the handkerchief that hid away her new big round yellow glasses. Clearing her hair away from her face, she then placed them gently upon her dainty fairy nose, all the while refusing to look at Blandine Buttercup.

There was a moment of silence. Blandine Buttercup hugged Daisydimple tightly and exclaimed at the top of her fairy voice.

"Daisydimple, you are a beautiful fairy and you are wearing the most magnificent pair of big round yellow glasses in the land." But most importantly was that Daisydimple could see clearly all around her now.

Back in the kitchen, the two fairies were doubled over from laughter. Their tummies ached as they rolled around the kitchen floor laughing at the muddled ingredients Daisydimple had previously gathered for pancakes.

Now, they were beating batter and tossing and flipping pancakes. Rapidly the scent of sugar-coated pancakes filled the air with bubbles that floated around and popped the delicious aroma under the fairy noses. The bubbles spread across the Fairy Dales and straightaway, the valley bell rang out loud, announcing to all the fairies that pancakes were ready.

One by one, the fairies arrived at Oak View Cottages. The gardens were decorated with colourful bunting and balloons and fruit juice and cream teas were served. On this wonderfully bright and warm day, the fairies watched as Blandine Buttercup arrived from the kitchen and into the garden with a tower of mouth-watering pancakes. Daisydimple followed, balancing her tray of wobbly pancakes and peering through her big round yellow glasses.

The Fairy Dales' fairies applauded. For the very first time, Daisydimple could see all of their fairy faces clearly, cheering and singing. They hadn't even noticed her new glasses sitting on the tip of her dainty button nose. Daisydimple believed them to be the best pair of big round yellow glasses in the land!

Chapter 3
Neddy Nettle and Betsy Bramble Steal the Fairy Dust

It was a dismal day in Fairy Dales. The clouds were heavy and low. The rain started falling on the quiet and empty little pathways. The birds preferred the shelter and the warmth of their cosy little nests, and the fairies chose to gather around their warm, crackling and glowing fires. Some fairies were baking yummy scones and chocolate cookies, whilst others liked sewing little bobble hats, mittens and socks to keep warm.

Betsy Bramble and Neddy Nettle were best friends. They lived in the North West of the Dales, in Bramble bush lodge. Stinging nettles and bramble bushes surrounded their home, so the other fairies never visited.

Both young fairies were quite mischievous, and rather naughty... Their idea of fun was to play tricks on the others.

On a cold and still morning, they were feeling bored so decided to venture out into the Dales to find something to do. Luckily, the fireflies were lighting up the Dales to help shine some light as the sun hid behind the bulky clouds.

Betsy and Neddy noticed that no other fairies were around, and this really bothered them. They wanted adventure.

Neddy had an idea. The one thing he loved above all else was Grandma Roseraine's fairy dust. It had always intrigued him, and as this day was so quiet, surely...

Neddy lead the way, and Betsy followed as a loyal best friend does. They thought about flying up all the way up to the old oak tree on the hilltop and stealing all of the precious petals from the rose bushes. If they did this, they would be able to collect Grandma Roseraine's fairy dust, and they could hide it in their treasure room at the bottom of Bramble Bush Lodge. In fact, the treasure room was full of stolen treasures...

So, laden with cotton bags, that is exactly what they did. They flew together up to the top of the hill, making sure they were careful not to be seen. Once at Grandma Roseraine's old oak tree, they tiptoed around, gently pulling off all of the petals off the bushes, as they filled their bags to the brim, leaving no trace of a single dropped petal behind. Swiftly, they swooped in the air and rapidly headed back home. Betsy Bramble and Neddy Nettle high-fived with glee the moment they closed their door. They danced around inside Bramble bush lodge. With two big fat smug faces and bags filled with petals, they were very happy with themselves.

"We must hide these in the treasure room very quickly!" Neddy hushed. "This is our most precious treasure of all."

As the night fell, and bedtime approached, Betsy and Neddy jumped into their beds and slowly closed their eyes. Because of all of the day's excitement and adventures, they were very tired, so very quickly they drifted off to sleep. The night passed, and the civil twilight gently appeared.

Six o'clock approached, and then... nothing. Grandma Roseraine was nowhere to be seen. No fairy dust trails. This could only mean one thing. This morning, it was silent. It was eerily silent and still. Not a single bird sang. The fairies didn't wake. The bees didn't buzz. Nothing. Just a very unusual stillness. This had never happened before in Fairy Dales.

Meanwhile, Betsy and Neddy casually yawned and stretched. They gradually woke up with no idea of what they had done. They slipped their miniscule feet into big fluffy slippers that looked like little marshmallows. The best friends grinned at each other, reminiscing on the previous day's adventures as they poked at their fire until it crackled and roared into action. The room warmed up quickly and smelt so delicious this morning. Just like a florist's dream.

Now that Grandma Roseraine's petals were at Bramble Bush lodge, they were filling the air with their magical aroma. Neddy Nettle and Betsy Bramble felt energised, lifted and ready for the day ahead. As Betsy glimpsed out of the window, she noticed that it hadn't become fully daylight, and that the famous Fairy Dales sundial seemed to have stuck on dawn.

Where are all of the other fairies? Betsy and Neddy thought to themselves. But this thought quickly shifted, and Betsy and Neddy were ecstatic. "Wait! This is amazing! The whole of Fairy Dales to ourselves!" they sung and cheered. "Let's go around to see what other mischief we can create today!" Neddy chanted, hopping from side to side. Betsy giggled with nervous excitement.

Off they flew, and their first stop was at Oak View cottages. When they peeked through the tiniest window, they saw Daisy Dimple sleeping, and decided to steal her beautiful and intricately hand-embroidered handkerchiefs. They flew across the town square and over to Bluebell Barn. They peeked in and saw Strawberryl's delicious, mouth-watering jams. So of course, they stole that too. They even flew all the way down to the Fairy Dales School and stole the head teacher's fragile and extremely rare crystal fairy globe.

They had lots of fun whilst the other fairies slept deeply. They quietly took it all back to their secret treasure room at Bramble Bush Lodge.

The rest of the day passed, night time came, and off to bed they went. Betsy was feeling a little afraid now, but tightly closed her eyes. During the night, she had many nightmares. The Dales was a little too quiet for her liking, and this made her feel very unsettled and worried.

Another night passed, morning approached, but once again, nothing... Silence. The sundial stayed at dawn. No birds sang, no bees buzzed and no sign of Grandma Roseraine. Fairy Dales continued to sleep.

Betsy and Neddy awoke once again but were not as smug as yesterday. They started to feel a little lonely. They didn't like the stillness of the Dales anymore. It was making them sad. They walked into the treasure room and stared at the bags full of petals with mixed emotions.

Neddy noticed that Betsy's eyes were filling up with sorry tears, so took it upon himself to try and fix this uncomfortable situation. He suggested that they fill their pockets with the stolen petals, which they both did straight away. They then headed out of the door, and flew over the Dales, throwing and scattering the petals in hope that this would wake the other fairies this morning.

But, despite their efforts, nothing. Fairy Dales was asleep and the petals didn't turn into Grandma Roseraine's famous fairy dust. This was dreadful.

With both of their heads bowed, dragging their wings, they slowly flew back home to Bramble Bush Lodge, feeling defeated. "What are we going to do now?" muttered Betsy. "We have done a terrible thing." Tears filled her eyes and started to roll down her cheeks. This made Neddy drop his head heavily into his hands with regret.

Grandma Roseraine could never make fairy dust without her petals, and this meant that Fairy Dales, would never wake again.

Suddenly, the realisation of what the pair had done overwhelmed them. "This is terrible!" they both squealed. "We must return the petals to Grandma Roseraine straight away!" Betsy ordered, wiping her eyes.

It took tremendous courage to fly all of the bags back up to the old oak tree. When they reached the hilltop, they saw Grandma Roseraine sitting on her little wooden rocking chair, just in front of her tiny crooked door, nestled away in the trunk of the enchanted oak tree. She was withered, fragile and looked very sad. She had lost the glowing rosy red colour in her cheeks. Her beautiful lace patterned wings were carefully tucked away behind her but refused to spread.

Betsy and Neddy advanced over to Grandma Roseraine, very slowly, with both of their heads facing the ground. As they reached the rocking chair, they both dropped to their knees like two sacks of potatoes in front of the elderly fairy, whimpering and apologising continuously. Over and over.

"Please forgive us, Grandma Roseraine."

"Please, please wake the Dales, it's so lonely, so quiet, and we are so scared and so sad."

"We are so, so, so, sorry. We love the fairy dust so much that we wanted to have it all. We didn't realise that the Dales would never wake again!"

Grandma Roseraine gently lifted her head, pushing her little half-moon glasses up onto her button nose so she could carefully acknowledge the heartfelt apologies that Betsy and Neddy offered. She reached out and took their hands gently into hers.

"If you both love fairy dust, I will make some extra fairy dust for you both, so that you may keep it in little jars in your house. But. In return, you will fly with me every morning to wake Fairy Dales. I will teach you how to sprinkle the magical fairy dust. You will learn, and you will become my little helpers." Grandma Roseraine was a very fair fairy.

She slowly stood with her eyes closed, breathing in the aroma from the returned rose petals, which energised her. She opened her little crooked door and buried into the trunk of the old oak tree, then hobbled inside. Betsy Bramble and Neddy Nettle followed, weighed down with the stolen bags of petals. Over the blazing fire, Grandma Roseraine went straight to work filling her cauldron and mixing her petals into fairy dust. Betsy and Neddy watched in complete awe. They had never seen something as beautiful as this before.

Rose petal perfume completely filled the room, making Betsy and Neddy heavy headed and giddy. The grandma fairy filled two little jars, as promised and handed them over to Betsy and Neddy. Then, once her baskets were filled with the fairy dust, they joined hands and swiftly flew into the air, gliding down to awaken the Fairy Dales of Alberton forest.

Somersaulting through the air above the tiny homes, they sprinkled the dazzling glittery dust. Suddenly, the Fairy Dales sundial started to creek as it began to work again. The sun gently rose and peeped over the horizon. Fairy noses twitched, the birds started to sing, and the bees started buzzing. Finally, the Fairy Dales awoke.

Betsy and Neddy were so overjoyed to finally see the valley bustling with activity again. However, one last thing was still on their minds. They had stolen other precious belongings from the fairies that needed to be returned.

They confessed to Grandma Roseraine, who in turn suggested that Betsy and Neddy were to invite all of the fairies to Bramble Bush Lodge for cream tea. This being the perfect occasion to apologise return all the stolen goods back to their rightful owners.

Betsy Bramble and Neddy Nettle had learnt a very important lesson.

Chapter 4
Applelena Blossom and Her Flute

The sun was glistening down onto Fairy Dales and the fresh blossom was in full abundance. Blossom Heights was a magnificent tree of dusty pink petals and was the home to two blossom fairies. Pinchpear and Applelena.

Applelena was a calm and shy little fairy. Her complexion was so pale, almost as white as a freshly fallen blanket of snow on a winter's day. She had long, immaculate ebony hair. She loved to paint and draw and did so perfectly. She was a very creative fairy.

Applelena however, had never mastered the art of reading and writing and she found it particularly difficult to speak too.

Applelena was as quiet as a mouse. She appeared to have no voice, so most of the time her long dark hair swallowed up her little face as she walked around the Dales, head down facing the ground. The other fairies didn't quite know how to include her in their daily activities or even playtime. They found her a little unusual and assumed that Applelena preferred to be left alone. This left Applelena feeling sorrowful, empty and sometimes quite lonely. Her little fairy feelings were aching and troubled. Pinchpear Blossom, who lived with Applelena was the only fairy who really knew and understood Applelena.

At Willow Woods, teacher Tabitha Tulip was organising her little home as part of her plan to help Applelena Blossom. She baked delicious chocolate chip cookies and carefully pressed juicy raspberries to make some juice. She set out an array of coloured paints, paper and a few musical instruments ready for the arrival of Applelena. Later that day, Applelena left Blossom Heights and in a flash, she flew across the Dales to Willow Woods. Applelena arrived with her books nestled under her arm and Tabitha welcomed Applelena with open arms. She was a caring fairy, so she made sure that the little apple blossom fairy felt comfortable.

Applelena began to form a lovely friendship with the teacher. She calmly created beautiful patterns and shapes in her attempt to explain her inner feelings. Tabitha was determined to understand, so she set out a plan.

"Dear blossom fairy, I am going to teach you to read notes and create sounds and melodies. It is called music. You will see that creating music is just like allowing paint to flow onto a canvas, which I know you love to do," the teacher said with enthusiasm.

Applelena Blossom lifted her head and briefly looked up at her teacher. Her beautiful angelic fairy face glowed with hope. Tabitha's heart warmed with emotion. They both eagerly started the lesson.

The days passed, and the weeks did too. Fairy Dales couldn't but notice Applelena Blossom flutter away daily over to Willow Woods, swinging her heavy books in her little apple green gingham bag below her, holding on to them tightly. Fairy Daphnedil who lived next door to Tabitha also noticed as she arrived daily. All of the inquisitive fairies in Fairy Dales whispered to each other and wondered how Applelena was progressing.

On one particular day, whilst Strawberyl was
delivering some of her mouth-watering berry
homemade jams to Daphnedil in Willow Woods, she
overheard a faint sound. As soon as Daphnedil
appeared at her door, Strawberyl shared this
with her and in one second, the two curious fairies
decided to creep over to Fairy Tabitha Tulip's
house with their ears wide open. As they sheepishly
approached the little cobbled pathway, the two
fairies stopped abruptly. They could hear the most
beautiful sound floating out of Tabitha's house.
They gasped, looked at one another with eyes as
wide as owl eyes. Their chins dropped as their
mouths opened in disbelief.

Magnificent, harmonious soft sounds of flute swirled the air and surrounded Strawberyl and Daphnedil, lifting them up as if they were swaying and twirling through fluffy clouds of sweet candyfloss. This was the most delicate sound of music that they had ever heard.

Briskly without waiting a moment more, they flew over to the little round window of Tabitha's house and glimpsed inside. Right there before their eyes, was Applelena Blossom with an exceptional, pearly silver flute gently cradled in her arms. There she stood, creating the most wonderful music with her tiny angelic fingers. Her eyes were lightly closed as her body swayed back and forth along with every note. Tabitha Tulip was right by her side watching with immense joy and admiration. She was the proudest fairy teacher in Fairy Dales.

Daphnedil and Strawberyl threw themselves into each other's arms, hugging each other tightly. Overwhelmed with bursting excitement, they flew off into the air. They just couldn't wait to share this special moment with the rest of the fairies in Fairy Dales.

They swooped straight down to the valley bell and pulled onto its ropes with all of their mighty weight and power. The bell chimed loudly, rippling echoes across the Dales, and rapidly all of the little confused fairies gathered into the town square to hear the exciting news that Daphnedil and Strawberyl were waiting to deliver.

Without a moment to take breaths, Daphnedil began to speak as Strawberyl added high-pitched squeals and excited little flutters of applause. In a flash, overwhelming emotion and pure elation took over Fairy Dales. The enthusiasm reached up to the top of the hill where Grandma Roseraine was tending to her roses bushes. She too, gracefully made her way down to join the group of fairies, accompanied by all of the shimmering fireflies. All together, they promptly flew over to Tabitha Tulip's house in Willow Woods.

Upon landing, they could hear the beautiful symphony that Applelena alone was creating. Every fairy wiggled and jiggled with fluttering wings as they energetically applauded. They wore the biggest smiles that Fairy Dales had even seen.

Applelena opened her eyes slowly, waking up from her trance and feeling a little confused. She could hear the cheers from the garden and decided to take a peek outside. She calmly pushed open the door and was soon faced with the most excited crowd of fairies ever. Holding her flute with both hands, she bent over and bowed shyly to her fellow fairy friends. The applause grew louder. Tabitha Tulip appeared behind the blossom fairy, guiding her out into the colourful, deliciously scented garden.

"Go on darling, Applelena!" she urged. "You have a wonderful gift, and the fairies would like you to share it with them. They have come to listen to the magical melodies that you alone are creating. Stand proud and shine like the brightest star in the sky."

Applelena lifted her head and looked deeply into Tabitha Tulip's eyes for the very first time. She felt strength and courage. She carefully positioned her flute, stood up straight, lifted her chin, rolled back her shoulders and as her eyelids slowly closed, she effortlessly began to sway once again, back and forth, side to side with every delicate note.

Her gift was truly magical. Applelena Blossom was a very special fairy.

Chapter 5
Pinchpear Blossom and the Lolly

It was a fine, sunny morning in Fairy Dales. The birds were whistling jolly tunes and the fairies were enjoying morning tea. There was a lot of humming and buzzing from the bees and Grandma Roseraine had not long passed over the Dales, sprinkling her fairy dust and waving to the fairies. Fairy Doctor Polly Iris was very busy in her surgery. She sang loudly as she spun around dancing whilst organising her lotions, syrups and potions neatly in her little glass cabinet. She didn't have the best of voices. It was more like yodelling.

"With a wheedle and a twiddle,
I take my needle,
With a splish, splosh, splash,
It's over in a flash.
No need to fear, let's stay jolly,
For there is a treat, a big red lolly."

Fairy Polly Iris was a short, very round, kind fairy with the tiniest feet. She fluttered her wings most of the time because it seemed as though she would fall over if she stood on them for too long. Her cheeks were like two juicy blueberries and her hair was as yellow as the yolk of a perfectly cooked egg. Her purple petticoats matched her purple hat. Between seasons, just as autumn crosses over to winter, Dr Polly Iris invited all of the fairies to come for a vaccination. This was to stop the flower fairies from wilting during the cold seasons.

Neddy Nettle, Betsy Bramble and Timmy Thistle didn't mind this day at all as they were used to prickles and stings. But, for the other fairies, just the thought made them shiver and quiver, frightening away their flower fairy colours. Many had flown up to the hilltop to visit the Comfort Tree to calm themselves.

There was one fairy in Fairy Dales whose knobbly knees were knocking and trembling louder than a foghorn. It was Pinchpear Blossom. He was usually a cheerful little fairy who carried a piper and would often be heard whistling jolly tunes. Pinchpear wore a green pear-shaped hat that curled slightly at the top and half covered his pointed fairy ears. His little boots were slightly tattered and torn from his dancing.

This was to be Pinchpear Blossom's very first vaccination and he was petrified. Inside his little tree house at Blossom Heights that he shared with Applelena Blossom, he had tossed and turned in his sleep all night long, and even had nightmares!
He was hiding under his little bed, but the tick tock of the clock rang louder and louder and Pinchpear Blossom became paler and paler. He tried to whistle some tunes, but they were just not coming out.
He paced every room in his house, back and forth. Applelena Blossom tried to cheer him up by playing her flute, but that didn't work either. He stopped and thought long and hard.
Rapidly, gathering himself and hugging Applelena, he closed his door behind him and flew off up to the top of the hill to the trunk of the old oak tree, where Grandma Roseraine lived. He could smell the beautiful roses as he approached and saw Roseraine appear at her tiny crooked door. She fluttered her wings wide and welcomed Pinchpear into her arms. Pinchpear Blossom needed no explanation. She sat him down on a squishy bed of rose petals and took hold of his hand.

"My dear, Pinchpear Blossom," she whispered softly, "I understand that you are afraid. We all become afraid of situations that we have never experienced before, but there really isn't anything to worry about. Everyone in the land has had a vaccination at some point and were probably nervous like you. It feels like a little tiny pinch that is all over in a flash. Doctor Polly Iris has a delicious treat for each fairy to enjoy as a reward for being such brave fairies. Come along Pinchpear Blossom. I will accompany you and give each fairy a little snuggle. Hugs are a marvellous remedy for nerves." Held close under Fairy Roseraine's wing, together they took off into the air, down the hill and to the surgery in the Dales Town Square. Pinchpear Blossom began to feel a whole lot better. He was thinking more about the delicious treat from Dr Polly Iris. Grandma Roseraine flew above in a circle and spread her wings wide, whilst Pinchpear held on gripping her waist. As she gently lowered to the ground, all the fairies swarmed close to greet and hug her. There was a lot of happiness and big smiles in the surgery today. Grandma Roseraine was spreading the joy and clapped a jolly tune. The fairies skipped from side to side and held hands. Even Dr Polly Iris yodelled along. She loved to flutter, dance and sing...

"With a wheedle and a twiddle, Polly takes her needle,
With a splish, splosh, splash, it's over in a flash,
Tick, tack, tock, here comes Polly,
With a treat in her pocket... It's our lolly."

Chapter 6
Gina Gerbera and Dotty Docleaf

Fairies are secretive. They hide in forest glades or on the leafy banks of rivers and streams. Fairy Gina Gerbera had two special fairy friends whom she loved to visit. They were called Fairies Snowdrop and Crimson Ivy. They lived just on the edge of Fairy Dales where the stream ran off to the sea. If you pay attention the next time you're out near the river, you may hear them chatting with the frogs and singing along with the birds. Wearing her red petal dress and matching hat, Gina left her house in Meadow View Manor and made her way to the edge of the valley, hopping and skipping whilst carrying a little woven basket full of plump, round fruity scones, some juice and a little red tartan blanket. She was joining Fairies Snowdrop and Crimson Ivy for a picnic.

hear the croaking of the frogs. They were singing along to the sweet melody of the birds. Fairies Snowdrop and Crimson Ivy could be faintly heard in the distance singing too.

"Small pebbles and
big pebbles,
All you have to do is follow
Mr Frog."

Gina joined in as she skipped towards the sounds, hopping from pebble to pebble along the stream and swinging her little basket to the tunes. Mr Frog appeared, "Croak, Croak," he jumped on to a pebble and led the way.

"Small pebbles and big pebbles, I shall take you to Snowdrop... Croak, croak."

In no time at all, the three fairy friends were together, having their picnic, playing hopscotch and hide and seek. But... Gina started very quickly to feel poorly hot and itchy. So, so hot and so, so itchy. She scratched and scratched from front to back. She itched and itched all over her body. Oh dear, poor Gina was covered in a rash. Red, spotty and hot, she bid farewell to her fairy friends and flew home and went safely to bed.

Wills Wallflower was a very tall, shy and sweet-scented fairy who lived with Gina Gerbera and Pansydee at Meadow View Manor in Fairy Dales. Wills noticed that Gina had rashes as red as her petticoats. So, he flew to the surgery in the town square to fetch Dr Polly Iris.

As fast as lightning, Dr Polly Iris arrived carrying lotions and potions to help her recover. She gave not one spoon, but two of potion and then covered poor Gina with lotion. Day one passed, then day two.

Wills Wallflower sat by her bedside day and night. There was nothing he could do but watch over her and wait. Slowly, the rashes disappeared and Gina stopped itching. She was feeling so much better now. On day four, Gina jumped out of her bed full of energy. She gathered up her little woven basket and once again filled it with fruity scones and juice.

This time, Wills was accompanying her for a picnic with fairies Snowdrop and Crimson Ivy. They left Meadow View Manor and flew over the Dales following the river that led to the sea. They landed on the riverbank. As they skipped along the bank, they could hear Mr Frog croaking his tune.

"Small pebbles and big pebbles... Croak, Gina is better, no more rash... Croak."

They could hear the birds singing, they heard Snowdrop and Crimson Ivy too.

"Big pebbles and small pebbles... Croak,
Gina and wills have brought a picnic... Croak."

Once again, the fairies played hopscotch and hide and seek, ate and drank juice and had a belly full of laughs together. Then, suddenly, Wills Wallflower and Gina Gerbera started to feel poorly, hot and itchy. So, so hot and so, so itchy. They scratched and scratched from front to back. They itched and itched all over their bodies. Poor Gina Gerbera and Wills Wallflower were both covered in a rash!

Mr Frog was jumping and splashing in and out of the water nearby and saw Gina and Wills jumping around itching and scratching. He stepped onto a pebble to take a closer look. The two fairies rolled around in the grass trying to soothe their itching. He knew just the right fairy to help. He started to croak loudly!

"Big pebbles and small pebbles,
Dotty Docleaf come at once...
Croak, croak,
Scratching and itching... Croak."

Dotty Docleaf flew along the stream to the bank where the other fairies were rolling about and quickly wrapped her arms around them. She enveloped her wings around them too, like a blanket, and hummed gentle words. Within a few seconds, Gina and Wills stopped itching. No more rash, no more scratching. It was like a magical potion. They all joined hands and danced. Mr Frog joined in too.

"Big pebbles and small pebbles... Croak,
Itching and scratching, it has stopped!
Dotty Docleaf is amazing,
No more rash, no more rash!
Croak, croak."

Chapter 7
Wills Wallflower and His First Day at School

The Fairy Dales Sundial had struck autumn, marking the end of the summer season. This meant that school was about to begin. The fairies were busy organising their daily duties from inside their little homes. Strawberyl and Bluebell Braie were at the bell tower in the valley town square pulling down on the ropes of the huge shiny bell. They did this with all of their strength, hanging from the ropes and jumping up and down like frogs. They were announcing to the other fairies the three new students that had been selected for school today.

You see, in Fairy Dales, the classroom was very tiny and could only fit three fairies at a time and lessons lasted only an hour. The rest of the fairies helped around the Dales with sewing and baking.

The big yellow sun was slowly rising, and the sky was as blue as the ocean, but it was a cold, crisp morning and the wind was bitter, sending chills through the dales. The grass crunched like cornflakes with every step of tiny fairy feet. The fairies put on their mittens, scarves and hats, wrapped up warm and braved the outside air. They gathered around the information board in the valley town square.

Wills Wallflower, a tall, shy fairy was there. He was a sweet scented, wild fairy with orangey, brown petals and green slippers. He was the most faithful of all fairies. Neddy Nettle stood next to Wills Wallflower and saw both their names clearly.

"I'm not ready," Wills whispered to himself. "I can't go, I'm scared of school. I'm shy, I'm not intelligent and what if I get everything wrong?" and the list went on and his brain became more and more frazzled.

Wills was crumbling like a biscuit, and he believed he was the only fairy feeling this way. Luckily, his friends Neddy, Nettle and Timmy Thistle also joining school today, were shaking until their leaves fell off.

Daphnedil, who was like a mummy fairy, had been busy during the Summer season cutting and sewing together little cotton, patchwork school bags for the fairies. She was a beautiful yellow fairy with her hair in a floppy white bun. She was always busy helping the other fairies.

Wills Wallflower was now worried that his little bag, full of pencils, might be too heavy to fly with. He felt sick, and his tummy was knotted, and his chin started to quiver.

Luckily, Timmy Thistle and Neddy Nettle flew over to Meadow View Manor to collect Wills on their journey to Fairy Dales School. All three fairies looked very smart as they crossed the valley to school carrying their little cotton bags.

The fairy bell chimed to announce the beginning of class. Neddy, Timmy and Wills lined one behind the other, very smartly, outside the Dales school for fairies they proceeded to enter the classroom and seated themselves facing Fairy Teacher Tabitha Tulip.

Tabitha welcomed them with the warmest and widest smile ever. The discussion this morning was focused around how the fairies were feeling about starting school today. Wills, Neddy and Timmy, all listened each in turn, attentively, and soon realised that knotted tummies and trembling knees were felt by each fairy that morning. Teacher Tabitha suggested that for the following day, each fairy should bring along a little keepsake from home to place on their desks. Perhaps a teddy or something they would like to snuggle for comfort.

All the fairies were over joyed with this and soon relaxed into their new class. It was an exciting time for Wills and his fairy friends. They had learnt of exciting and interesting lands outside of Fairy Dales, they were taught that Grandma Roseraine's old oak tree was enchanted, and even learnt about the magical powers of the school fairy globe. They flew home together discussing how they would meet up the following morning for school. They all agreed that school was fun, learning was fun, and they couldn't believe they even had milk and cookies at the end of the day!

Chapter 8
Pansydee and the Loose Tooth

It was a rather chilly, frosty morning and the glorious sun had decided to stay hidden behind the large, fluffy and white clouds. The flower fairies didn't like the frost, it made them shiver. They definitely preferred the warmer toastier days for sure.

Most of the fairies were in the warmth of their little homes, devouring porridge for breakfast whilst sitting by their cosy fires and taking note of their duties for the day ahead.

Pansydee was a flamboyant and colourful fairy. Her long red hair was braided all the way down to her waist. She lived in Meadow View Manor on the east side of Fairy Dales with her two fairy friends; Gina Gerbera and Wills Wallflower.

On this particular morning, something was occupying her thoughts. Her little face was troubled. Pansydee hadn't eaten breakfast and this was unusual as she loved her toasted bread with butter. Gina and Wills were at the breakfast table, looking rather concerned. Pansydee seemed to have lost her appetite. She even refused to brush her teeth.

Pansydee had a very wobbly loose tooth. It was so wobbly that it moved from left to right and front to back every time she spoke. Pansydee was so worried that it may fall out, that she decided to keep her mouth tightly closed.

What if she yawned and swallowed it? What if she spoke and dropped it? What if this tooth fell out and all the other teeth followed...

How could she possibly fly to school? She thought. She risked losing her tooth way down across the Dales, on rooftops or in the fields below. It could fall anywhere, and she would lose it forever.

So, Pansydee decided to walk to school, keeping her little fairy feet firmly on the ground. Oh no, Pansydee had forgotten something very important. It was the coldest, frostiest morning ever and Pansydee's teeth began to chatter. And chatter they did, very loudly indeed! They chattered all the way to school, chattered at school and continued to chatter all the way home again. The whole of Fairy Dales could hear.

Pansydee hurried her little feet home as fast as she could. Her whole body began to shiver and shake as she crossed the valley town square and through the little cobbled pathways, to Meadow View Manor.

She opened her little gate and trotted rapidly down her pathway, but just before entering her tiny red door, her friend Fairy Timmy Thistle flew by whistling down to her.

"Coming for tea, Pansydee? Hot chocolate muffins!" he cried.

She glanced up at Timmy Thistle fluttering above her in the air and as she opened her mouth to reply, her little wobbly tooth catapulted against her tiny red door.

Pansydee yelped in horror and threw herself to the ground, fluttering and flapping as she frantically searched for her fallen tooth.
"I've lost my tooth, Timmy," she murmured with a quivering voice.
Timmy Thistle whisked past and landed right next to the lonesome tooth. He laughed out loud.
"Don't be afraid! Everyone loses a tooth. I've already lost three!" he said proudly as he proceeded to open his mouth and show her.
"It means you are growing Pansydee." But Pansydee was still worried.
"What am going to do with it now and how am I going to glue it back inside my mouth?" she whimpered.
"You don't have to glue it back Pansydee," laughed Timmy,
"Another tooth will grow in its place. The stronger tooth has pushed the little one out. Haven't you heard of Peggy the tooth fairy from the Tooth Fairy Land?"

Timmy continued...
"Well, tonight when you go to bed, you must wrap your little tooth in a handkerchief and place it under your pillow before you sleep. During the night, Peggy the tooth fairy will come and take your tooth away. In Tooth Fairy Land, they use them to build their castles. She will thank you by leaving a gleaming penny in its place."
Pansydee's face beamed and her cheeks flushed as red as her hair. She was excited that her little tooth will be of use to the tooth fairy. And a gleaming shiny penny would be given in return!
"Of course, I shall come for tea and hot chocolate muffins Timmy. That sounds delicious!"

Chapter 9
Fairy Dales and the Sundial

As quick as the fairy noses twitched, they were all jumping out of bed and fluttering around with excitement. Each fairy had a duty. Some were baking scones and preparing sandwiches, others were tying balloons and ribbons together. The valley fireflies were checking their lights too so that they shone as bright as stars.

It was the first day of spring and the fairies were organising a spring fayre. The root fairy family were due to arrive, to join in with the celebrations. The Dales was bustling with activity and cheer. In the very centre of the Fairy Dales town square was a beautiful lake, filled with water flower fairies, toads and frogs. They too, were excited. And on the edge of this lake, directly in line with the hilltop to the old oak tree, sits the Fairy Dales sundial. This was closely watched by all.

Little food wagons were placed around the field near the lake and decorated with balloons and bunting. Towers of sandwiches were laid on china plates, and scones and fruit tarts were sending delicious puffs of steam into the air, from being still hot from the oven.

Fairy Strawberyl had her little food wagon filled with her mouth-watering jams to accompany the scones. Fairies were flittering about so quickly and energetically that if you blinked, you would miss them. Excitement was everywhere, and Fairy Dales was looking glorious.

Applelena Blossom was carefully cleaning her flute. She was going to entertain the fairies with some wonderful tunes, and Teacher Tabitha Tulip was close by her side.

The maypole was standing proud, with rainbow coloured glittery ribbons attached to the top.

The ribbons were flowing in the breeze creating sparkles all over the Dales. The landscape had transformed. It was the most colourful, vibrant and magical land the fairies had ever seen.

The Fairy Dales Bell rang loudly as the root fairies flew into the valley. Everyone cheered as they landed. Fairy Pansydee was flittering about, serving the cream teas and sandwiches. All the fairies then gathered around overlooking the Fairy Dales Lake, chatting and laughing excitedly, whilst enjoying the food.

The bell chimed once again, and silence fell.
Everyone stopped and watched.
Grandma Roseraine gracefully sprinkled rose
petals around the huge sundial and Applelena
delicately started to play her flute.
As the sun rose gently, its rays crept slowly across
the sundial, lighting it up. The sundial then creaked
and pointed to spring. Suddenly, the sunrays shone
brightly over the lake. The lake awoke.
Water funnels spouted up high, creating sounds
of panpipes with every gush. The frogs and toads
started to croak in unison as the water flower
fairies swam in circles, creating patterns across
the lake.
The sun now reached its peak in the sky with its
rays dancing up to the top of the valley hill, bathing
the old oak tree in warm sunlight. It shone as bright
as the brightest star in the sky.
Applelena Blossom played her flute louder and
Pinchpear Blossom joined her with his piper.
The birds whistled along too. The fairies danced
around the maypole as the fireflies flew above,
twinkling brightly. The celebrations of spring
continued all through the day and night.
The long-awaited Season had arrived.

Chapter 10
Fairy Dales and the Bah Humbugs

Little petals of white snow fell silently and gently down over Fairy Dales all through the night. It covered the fairy homes like a soft blanket of marshmallows and candyfloss. The young fireflies laid cosily inside their warm cocoons with their lights on, perfectly cradled on top of the twigs that lined the little cobbled pathways lighting the way. They gleamed brightly as the snow fell.

Grandma Roseraine wrapped herself in warm clothes and braved the cold outside as she loyally completed her duties. She flew down over the Dales scattering her rose petal fairy dust to wake the valley.

The first robins sang, and little fairy lights began to twinkle from the fairy windows. Each fairy stretched and yawned and enveloped themselves warm in winter clothing. They slipped their fairy feet into big fluffy warm slippers and headed to the fireplace to keep warm.

It was Christmas Eve and time for all the fairies to huddle together and fly up to the hillside to Fairy Eden Evergreen's house. She lived inside the hill to the East of the Dales, hidden away behind a little green door. Behind this door, a small hallway led to a cosy kitchen. Another, led the way to a beautiful garden full of miniature evergreen trees. These two rooms were Eden's favourite places. She took extra care all year round to tend to her trees in preparation for Christmas.

Grandma Roseraine rang the Fairy Dales Bell. The fairies huddled in a group, each holding a large leaf above their heads to shelter them from the falling snow. The bell then rang a second time, announcing the procession led by the fireflies up into the sky and high above the Dales to Eden's house. They could see a warm glow shining across the hillside from Eden Evergreen's open door where she awaited with hot chocolate as they arrived. Strawberyl and Bluebell Braie didn't know what all the fuss was about. Christmas was not special to them and they didn't believe in Santa anyway! Strawberyl dragged her feet as the other fairies fluttered happily through to the kitchen.

A very excited bunch of fairies were greeted with the heavenly smell of homemade cooking and a tray full to the brim of mince pies that Eden had baked early that morning. Strawberyl's eyes lit up. This was definitely the best part of this Christmas Eve. She then proceeded to tuck into the mountain of pies. Bluebell Braie closely by her side, joined her, making sure he didn't drop a single crumb. The fairies gathered their little trees from Eden's garden and laid them onto a net that the fireflies lifted into the air and transported back to the valley. They all bid farewell to Eden Evergreen and flew through the falling snow, back down into Fairy Dales.

Strawberyl and Bluebell Braie were in their little house at Bluebell Barn, trying to get excited for the upcoming festivities. They poked around at the fire to light it up. This was proving to be quite challenging. It just did not work. They tried everything. Strawberyl had to wear extra woolly jumpers now to keep warm. She was shivering. Firefly Fred arrived with their Christmas tree, carrying it into the kitchen and placing it on the little windowsill ready to be decorated. He could see that Strawberyl and Bluebell were struggling to light the fire and wondered for a moment. These two adorable fairies really were in a pickle. Firefly Fred took the poker and sang Christmas carols as he blew onto the wood, until the fire roared back with bright orange flames. As he handed the poker back to Strawberyl, the fire started to die again.

Firefly Fred wondered again. *Maybe these two little fairies need to help me with my Christmas tree deliveries and start to believe in Santa and the Christmas season,* he thought.

They needed to feel the true Christmas spirit. So, wrapped up warm, with mittens and bobble hats, they travelled to Oak View Cottages, Blossom Heights, Bramble Bush lodge and Meadow View Manor with Firefly Fred, delivering the carefully chosen Christmas trees.

Jolly Christmas cheer and music was heard from each home. The gorgeous smell of steamed Christmas puddings and the twinkling of fairy lights and hot, blazing firesides welcomed the two fairies with Firefly Fred.

Strawberyl and Bluebell Braie sang along to Christmas carols and joined in on the piano. Fred danced around the trees, layering them with baubles and lights. They shared tales of Christmas adventures and drank warm frothy milk. Strawberyl and Bluebell were jolly. They could feel the Christmas cheer buzzing through their bodies and fairy wings, right down to their fairy feet. Christmas lights were twinkling brighter than ever before.

The night approached, and the valley was shining gloriously. Firefly Fred returned home to his cocoon in the old oak tree. Where he laid down straight into his bed, feeling rather worn out.
Strawberyl and Bluebell Braie were now home too, in pyjamas and very excited. Their little house at Bluebell Barn was warm and cosy, and the fire was finally roaring. They joined hands and danced around the kitchen singing at the tops of their voices. It echoed across the valley and reached up to the old oak tree where Firefly Fred could hear. He smiled to himself as he closed his eyes and turned on his light. His work was completed. Fairy Dales twinkled to sleep, and the festive season had begun.

The End